If Only Love was Enough

NAMRATA GUPTA

If Only Love was Enough

NAMRATA GUPTA

KALAMOS LITERARY SERVICES LLP

Kalamos Literary Services LLP
Email: info@kalamos.co.in | editorial@kalamos.co.in
Published in 2021 by
Kalamos Literary Services
ISBN- 978-93-90909-14-8

If Only Love was Enough 2021
Namrata Gupta

Typeset in Kalamos Litrary Services LLP

Cover designed by Brand Inspire OPC Pvt. Ltd.

Print and bound in India.

Lord of the Drinks, Connaught Place. I checked out the rosy pink lipstick on my heart shaped lips in the mirror of the share cab as I reached the café. In all the 23 years of my existence, I still hadn't perfected the art of applying a winged eyeliner on my round eyes. After countless experiments of various styles, I had figured that long layers suited my long oval face the best and I had been sticking to that haircut since a year and a half.

It had been three months since I started singing at Lord of the Drinks on the Live Music days every fortnight but even then, every time I began playing my guitar, a chill would run through me like it was the first time I was entertaining a live audience. I entered the premises at 8 pm sharp on a Friday, carrying my guitar and throwing my frizzy hair around. It wasn't that the crowd rose and cheered for me as soon as I entered. On the contrary, I was the one looking around to check out the numbers. There was a substantial head count and people were still coming in. I kept walking towards the stage with a racing heartbeat.

As I unpacked my guitar on reaching the chair kept vacant for me at the center of the stage, I began telling myself, 'Come on, Ridhima! Nobody knows you here. Half of the people would be too drunk to care about how you sing. It's fine as long as you play the popular passionate tracks. Nobody will recognize you if you run into them in a supermarket so what's the big deal if you don't sing well! There's nothing to lose.'

Reassuring myself with such thoughts like I was a frightened little kid who had been asked to sing a poem on stage during the assembly, I sat on the chair and looked around for one last time before I started playing the guitar.

'And of course, it's not as if Rahul is here.'

Rahul was the guy I had a crush on since my college days but he saw me only as a good friend. His presence would have made me weak in the knees but he never had the time to come to a café while I was playing there. Most of the time, he was busy impressing Deeksha, his crush and the only girl he seemed to care about. He fought the world for her. If anything hurt her, he made sure that it didn't make her sad again. Seeing him fight for her would boil my blood to a torturous degree.

'I wish I was Deeksha,' I thought.

The chain of thoughts had created the suitable aura for me to pour my heart out. I was hurt again, and thus, it was time for me to start playing to vent out the pain that would otherwise be buried deep within me.

Giving voice to my pain, I began playing my version of *Can't Help Falling in Love* by Elvis Presley.

'Take my hand, take my whole life too...' I began.

I had to sing for an hour. Thirty minutes into the performance, I looked at the crowd holding their glasses up to me while the chorus for the next song played. Some people clapped and cheered for me while others looked into the eyes of their beloved while holding their hands. Amongst the faces was a familiar face. It was a guy who looked in his late twenties sitting at a table in my diagonal line of sight on the right-hand side. I had often seen him sitting at the same table while I played, always smiling at me whenever I looked around.

As the chorus stopped, I channeled my inner pain to give voice to my wounds once again.

As my performance ended, I waved to the management and left the premises. I shared a cab with a fellow passenger and reached my house at 9:30 pm.

As I entered my house, I kissed my dad's photograph kept on the side table of my bed. Then, I held my mom's photograph placed beside it, into my hand, ran my fingers across her cheeks and kissed her too.

I hugged the two photographs close to my chest as if I was hugging both of them.

I had lost my dad due to a major heart attack three years ago and my mom had left me five years ago as she failed to fight stomach cancer. And so, coming back home to my parents after a bad day wasn't an option for me. I wished I could hug my mom once again when I was too tired to hold my broken pieces together but no matter how badly I wanted to do it, I couldn't. Tears weren't enough to bring my parents back.

After putting the photographs back on to the side table, I laid down on my bed and began scrolling through my phone. The news of the contagious and deadly Coronavirus spread like wildfire as the tally of the total number of live Covid-19 cases in India reached 1300. Out of these 1300 cases, 500 cases were live in Delhi-NCR itself. The virus could be transferred to another person by touching or shaking hands or just breathing around them, which made masks and hand sanitizers essential. It could stay on the surfaces for sanitizing the surroundings became important.

As I ate my dinner, I kept looking at my phone anticipating a call from Rahul. But my love wasn't enough to make him miss me.

Being disappointed, I took my guitar and began practicing a new song. The song failed to heal me. I kept my guitar back, laid down on my bed and kept looking at Rahul's WhatsApp display picture as it made me feel closer to him.

As the feeling of emptiness engulfed me, I switched off all the lights in my 2BHK house except one as it made the house look less creepy when I woke up in the middle of the night, and closed my eyes to imagine Rahul's face.

I woke up the next morning with the ringing alarm. I rushed to the kitchen after freshening up. Another failed attempt at making the ginger tea just like my mom did, made me mutter 'I miss you, mom' as I sipped the tea.

I was soon caught up in the daily humdrum as I wasn't able to make the ends meet by a meagre income from doing live performances. Following my passion instead of working in a traditional 9 to 5 job was getting heavy on my pocket as the daily expenses made sure that I was left with no savings at the end of the month. I was living hand to mouth. But I had decided to give my passion one last chance by starting a YouTube channel and being active on social media in the hope of becoming a social media sensation someday. I had given myself three months' time, post which I had to prepare myself for a regular 9 to 5 job.

After taking a few sun-kissed selfies with the right amount of cleavage showing up, I set up my camera and began recording.

***

The Covid-19 tally had crossed 10,000 live cases in Delhi itself. The virus was spreading at an unanticipated fast rate. After fifteen days of my last live performance, I received calls from the management of the cafés I used to play at telling me that live performances were cancelled until further notice. As a child who had lost both of her parents to different diseases, another deadly virus couldn't scare me. I wanted to perform despite the outbreak and pleaded the management to let me do it but to no avail.

All my hopes of surviving the upcoming two months with enough money vanished when the Prime Minister imposed a three-week lockdown due to the lack of medical resources needed to combat the outbreak. Like others, I rushed to the nearby grocery stores after checking my supplies. People were gathered in the grocery stores like swarms of flies, shouting the names of the items they needed at the top of their voice. I managed to get inside the third closest grocery store as it was a little less crowded than others but was disappointed on realizing that it was less crowded only because it had exhausted its supplies of the essential items.

"1000 for sugar! Last packet!" the retailer shouted.

'Black marketing, seriously?' I thought and took a deep breath.

Two days had passed since the lockdown had been imposed. It was 12 am when I was scrolling through Instagram where people posted new stories every two hours to keep the followers abreast with what they were up to. Mundane day-to-day activities were being showcased like achievements. Following the trend, I put up stories paying tribute to my culinary skills as well, but it was an activity that I engaged in every day. It was just in these unusual times that I thought of displaying it on social media.

I was wondering how social media had reduced people to profiles, shaping our judgement about them, the life they lead, their character, personality, looks and achievements and thus, reducing all the years of their life to a series of posts, when I received a message request from a profile that had been following me.

'Hey, I am Armaan. I've been attending your live music events at Lord of the Drinks on Fridays. Ever since I attended the first event, I haven't missed any Friday. There's something about your voice that heals me and gives me solace, and the lockdown is giving me a pretty hard time. I was wondering if you would like to sing exclusively for me over Zoom calls? Payments are not an issue. Please let me know. Thanks.' Read the message.

I kept my phone aside, not knowing what I wanted to say in reply and if I wanted to do it. The lockdown and Rahul's unresponsiveness had taken a toll on my peace of mind. After thinking for half an hour, I replied to Armaan.

'Hi, Armaan! Glad to know that you like my voice. Can you please tell me about the commercials and how often you would like me to play for you? Also, just to bring to your notice, recording or using the video/song/music in any form wouldn't be allowed. You can't post it anywhere.'

In a few seconds, I received his reply, 'No issues! I won't use the video/song/music anywhere and you can turn off recording. I would like to start with twice a week, Wednesday and Saturday. You can quote your price.'

Surprisingly, he didn't negotiate on the commercials and was ecstatic to know that I would be playing exclusively for him. His elatedness presented a sharp contrast to Rahul's disinterest in attending my live shows.

The messages from Armaan overwhelmed me. Although, I was the girl who people raised a toast to and now, wanted to sing just for them, I still wasn't the girl Rahul loved. I was incomplete even with my talents and Deeksha was complete even without them. She was a lucky woman. She had Rahul.

As I was lost in my chain of thoughts, my phone beeped again.

'Please sing a song that you haven't sung for anyone before.' It read.

I was immediately reminded of the song that I had prepared for Rahul. I had reserved it especially for him. I wanted to sing it for him under a star lit sky with nobody around us. But, he never had the time.

I shared my bank account details with Armaan. He wanted me to play for him on the coming evening.

I tried to practice different songs throughout the day but couldn't sing anything as perfectly as I could sing the song that I had reserved for Rahul. Not wanting to disappoint my client and being hopeless about Rahul making time for me, I decided to go ahead with it.

I was dressed up in a long navy blue cotton maxi with my hair untied. I had applied basic make-up to look good on the camera. Armaan joined the meeting at the scheduled time.

I was curious to see the guy who claimed to be a fan of my voice. His Instagram posts didn't help me in that regard because they didn't have any photograph that showed his face clearly. It was either his back or an edited picture that had found a place amidst nature on his feed.

He turned on his camera. After some thought, I could place him as the guy who always used to sit at the same table, smiling at me while I played at Lord of the Drinks. A little stubble complimented his square face with cupid bow lips and almond eyes. He had noticeably long and thick eyelashes which I started adoring the moment I set my eyes on them.

"Ready?" he asked in a husky voice.

I confirmed and began singing with my eyes closed.

I sang for 45 minutes, not thinking about anything else except the lyrics. It was the first time in many years that I was in the moment while singing. Otherwise, I always used to think about Rahul whenever a song ended.

Armaan didn't interrupt me with additional requests while I was singing.

"So which was the song that you haven't sung for anyone before?" he asked.

"The first one, *Tujhe Kitna Chahne Lage Hum* from Kabir Singh," I said.

"Well sung! What a passionate beginning!" he said.

"I hope I could make the evening worth your while," I said.

"Absolutely. I hope we're meeting on Saturday next?" he asked.

I replied in the affirmative.

"By the way, you look beautiful today," he said, smiling.

I thanked him and smiled back.

While I was cooking dinner for myself, the payment for 6 sessions was credited to my account. I thanked Armaan for paying in advance.

'I can't get your voice out of my head. It plays in my head like a record on loop. By the way, I hope I didn't cause any inconvenience to your family by my request.' He pinged.

'I live alone. I lost both of my parents a few years ago.' I replied.

'I am so sorry. How did that happen?' He asked.

'My mom had a stomach cancer and my dad passed away due to a major heart attack.' I replied.

'Okay. That's extremely sad. I'm sorry for your loss.' He replied.

'So, are you a trained singer?' He sent another message.

'Yes, I did take some classes.' I replied.

'Where all do you sing?' He asked.

I sent him the names of all the different cafés I played at regularly, along with the day and timings.

'Good to know. Earlier, I used to visit Lord of the Drinks every Friday because I didn't want to miss any evening. But later, I asked the waiter and he told me that you sing every fortnight. Now I know where else to find you.' He wrote and added a happy smiley.

'Where do you put up?' I asked.

'I'm from Himachal. I am employed in graphic designing in Delhi. I put up in Janakpuri.' He replied.

'So, are you in Himachal right now?' I asked.

'No, I'm stuck in Delhi. I couldn't go home as the lockdown was declared at the last moment. But it's fine. I'm working from home these days.' He said.

'Oh, so you live all alone?' I asked.

'Yeah. And what do you do apart from singing?' He asked.

'Nothing as of now. But will have to switch to a job soon.' I replied.

'Why?' He asked.

'Financial problems. The income is unstable and I live hand to mouth. I end up with no savings at all. I guess I'll have to compromise on my passion a bit.' I replied.

'Don't tell me you would stop singing! You have the power to heal people with your voice.' He said.

'Haha! I can't even heal myself with my voice.' I replied, adding a chuckling smiley.

'I'm serious. Please don't ever give up singing. People like me need your talent to get through life.' He wrote.

'I'll be glad if I can be of help. Are you looking out for more options for a stable income?' He asked.

'Well, I'm working on improving my social media presence and building my YouTube channel. Let's see how it goes.' I wrote.

'Yeah, you can work on female covers. Your cover of *Can't Help Falling in Love* by Elvis Presley that you sang at Lord of the Drinks was melodious. I think your talent will eventually reach the right audience. Focus on the female covers for a start. You can sing them for me and practice. I'll give you an honest feedback. Also, I can create some beautiful posts for social media which you can post regularly to earn more followers.' He said.

'Thank you so much.' I replied.

'We are both alone in our homes in the lockdown. Let's help each other grow and heal.' He wrote.

'Yes, surely.' I said.

'I'll design and share the posts with you. I can also design the thumbnail of your YouTube videos and help you in editing them. Meanwhile, please work on the female covers. You have the potential. I don't want you to remain undiscovered. You're a gem!' He said.

'You're very kind. Your words have infused me with a new hope.' I replied.

I practiced singing some covers and mixed them in my playlist when I sang for Armaan on Saturday. He liked them very much. Armaan sent me two posts to be uploaded on the weekend. He also edited my first *Can't Help Falling in Love* cover video and I uploaded it on YouTube on Sunday.

He shared the link on all his social media platforms and asked his friends to do the same. Within an hour, 15 profiles shared the video link. His network helped me increase my reach.

'You're helping me so much. Is there anything I can help you with?' I pinged Armaan.

'Yes, please never stop singing. And please teach me how to make atta halwa. I'm craving it.' He said.

'Haha! Will do.' I replied.

The next evening, Armaan took me on a video call while he made atta halwa as per my instructions.

"Keep stirring it otherwise you will burn the atta," I said, as Armaan placed his phone at the right angle using a holder on the wall during our WhatsApp video call.

"I'm tired. I've been stirring it since so long! How long does it take?" he said.

I laughed and said, "Just ten minutes more."

He pinged me later in the night.

'I can't sleep. Sing for me, please?' He wrote.

'I can't sleep either. It's 3 am and you want me to sing for you. Are you crazy?' I replied.

'No, but I might go crazy if I don't hear you singing right now.

Pleaaaaaaaaaaase.' He requested.

'Dude?' I replied.

'What's the big deal? Just pick up the guitar and get on a video call.' He replied.

'Alright, send me the meeting link.' I said.

I got up, untied my hair, picked up the guitar and opened the meeting link.

"Wow! You look gorgeous. You look so pretty without any make-up. And your hair! Those loose strands falling on to your face and shoulders, how adorable! Wait, let me go to my balcony. Stars and you, what a sight!" he said.

I blushed.

I sang for him sitting on my bed in my PJs. I wasn't looking pretty at all in the mirror.

But after singing for him, I realized that I had started living in the moment more. Earlier, I lived in my head with Rahul's memories and thoughts occupying my mind space every time. But now, I was able to focus on just the lyrics when I sang. I was not absent-minded while having a conversation with Armaan. I had finally begun to be at the same place mentally as I was physically. I didn't think of Rahul when a song ended anymore. I instead focused on the next song.

It was the second week of lockdown and the death anniversary of my mother. I woke up to some memes from Armaan at 5 am. I paid my respects to my mother and made arrangements for the rituals to be carried out during the day.

I received a message from Armaan stating that we would have the Zoom call an hour later as an urgent mid-week meeting had come up. This time I decided not to dress up for the virtual singing session, partly because I was too tired and partly because something within me told me that it wouldn't matter to Armaan as he liked me how I was.

"Before you begin singing, tell me if you slept last night because you replied to my messages at 5 in the morning," he said.

"Actually, it's my mother's death anniversary today so I had to make some arrangements for the rituals," I answered.

"Oh! So were you able to carry out the rituals smoothly? Or the lockdown didn't let you?" he asked.

"It was difficult, but I managed. Everything is done now," I replied.

"Okay," he said.

He noticed that I was getting a bit sad so he said, "I can understand it might get lonely sometimes, living all alone. But you can talk to my mother whenever you miss your mom. I know she can't replace her but it might help. My mom's pretty cool!"

I smiled and said, "That's very kind of you. I'm sure she's cool. But won't she think that there's something going on between us?"

"No, no. I'll handle it, don't worry. I video call her every day. Let me know if you want to join in some day," he said.

"For sure! Thanks!" I replied.

I sang a song that I was going to record that night amongst others.

"I'll record *Iktara* tonight," I said, after the 45 minutes session ended.

"Nice! What time?" he asked.

"12 am maybe," I replied.

"Why so late?" he asked.

"It's difficult recording during the day due to the background noises. At night, there's no noise, everything's calm and the mood is just right," I said, winking.

He smiled.

"But I can't figure out what to wear! Can you help me?" I asked.

"Sure," he said.

"Alright, time for a sneak peek into my waaaaaaardrobe," I sang.

I showed him a couple of dresses. He liked gowns, skirts and evening dresses the most. We shortlisted three attires for different recordings as per the song I had in mind. All of them were pastel shades.

"Wear this when we meet," he said, pointing to an off-shoulder pastel pink dress.

"Oh, so are we meeting?" I asked.

"Yes, of course. Won't you like to meet me when the lockdown ends?" he asked.

"Yeah," I replied.

'Done with the recording?' He texted me at 2 am.

'Yes. What's up?' I asked.

'I can't sleep.' He said.

'Me neither.' I replied.

'Umm… Would you like to go to Norway with me?' He asked.

'Haha! Yes, right now.' I joked.

'Let's take you there then!' He replied, adding a smirking smiley.

'Can't wait!' I joked.

After 5 minutes, he sent me a Zoom meeting link and asked me to open it on my laptop. I did as instructed and he shared his screen.

"Okay, so before I begin, I want you to video call me using your phone so that I can see your face while you watch what I'll just show you," he said.

I did as he said.

"Perfect! Now let me share my screen," he said.

He played a live video of aurora borealis.

"Clear March end night skies," he said on the WhatsApp video call.

I was mesmerized to see the green and red flames of light stretch across the sky forming a glowing curtain of light forms, waving and swirling before my eyes. The dancing flames lasted for a few minutes.

"Wow! It was so beautiful… so overwhelming… out of this world," I said.

"And it was a live video. So, you watched the aurora borealis live with me. Wow!" he said.

I smiled.

"By the way, the look on your face was equally priceless. My personal aurora borealis!" he said.

I blushed.

He laughed as he saw me blushing.

"Good night, beautiful! Go sleep now," he said, and cut the call.

April had begun. The weekend witnessed the first April rain. The rains had something beautiful and sad about them. While it was sheer joy to watch the tiny droplets of water fall on different surfaces, it left behind a feeling of emptiness when it stopped pouring. It was akin to how some people walk into our lives, making us brim with joy while they stay with us like the pouring rain and leaving us with an inexplicable sorrow when they leave. It's ironic how it is often said that life goes on despite everything when it can actually be the saddest part to go on without someone who was the reason why you wanted to live in the first place.

I didn't feel like singing that day. It was one of those days when I felt lifeless, like there was no soul in my body. My body seemed like just a dead weight lying on the bed, too heavy to get up.

Armaan understood that I needed a break from our virtual singing session that day. Wanting to help me, he coaxed me to meditate.

"Just for 15 minutes," he said. "It'll be fun. Please, please, pleaaaaaase."

"Alright, but just 15 minutes!" I said.

"Promise," he said.

To help me focus, Armaan played a video showcasing the sounds made by the planets. He asked me to keep my eyes closed and meditated with me.

While Mercury made purring and strong wind noises, Venus played a ritual music. Earth sounded like laser fights, Saturn sounded like the voice of the damned souls and Jupiter sounded like the intense eerie music played in a horror movie.

"Oh my god! What did I just hear!" I exclaimed after the session.

"Haha! How was it?" he asked.

"Intriguing! You really are into astronomy," I said.

"Not relaxing? And yeah, I do want to own a telescope someday," he said.

"Yes, it was relaxing too. And I like your plans!" I said.

"Then, we'll look at the galaxies together," he said.

I smiled and said, "We haven't even met!"

"We have! Just virtually!" he said, winking.

It was the third week of the lockdown. Unfortunately, I had failed to become a social media sensation and *Can't Help Falling in Love* cover YouTube video had just crossed 1k views. That reality put a halt to all the racy thoughts I had about my future.

"Come on, Ridhima! You have just started! It takes time," Armaan consoled me over the video call.

"Now was the best time and this was the last hope," I said.

"Ridhima, it hasn't been even a month. Calm down," he consoled.

"I'm not making any videos now. Fuck it! I cannot fight the reality. Living in the world of your dreams doesn't change the reality. And dare anybody talks about manifestation again!" I said angrily.

"Patience, my lady," he consoled.

"Fuck patience! This is the real world. The world where there are no miracles. Miracles, my foot! Blessings, lol! And manifestation, what crap!" I shouted.

As Armaan was helping me calm down, his doorbell rang.

"Wait a minute. Be on the call," he said.

He rose from his chair and opened the door. I could see him talking to someone. Then, he rushed back to his laptop and told me that he would call me later.

He called me after half an hour.

"I'm so sorry. It was my neighbor. Uncle's pretty old. He hurt himself while cooking food and had come to ask for a band aid. I had gone to his house to help him a bit," he said.

"Oh, so he lives alone?" I asked.

"Yeah, his children live abroad. Now that maids are not coming for work, he has to manage everything by himself," he said.

"Oh, I see," I said.

"He is really nice. He drops by whenever he feels like talking to someone. If he cooks something delicious, he gets it for me. I help him with menial tasks. I check up on him every now and then," he said.

"Like I always say, you're very kind," I said, smiling.

Later in the evening, I sent Armaan some pictures while making different weird faces. The collar of my shirt and my posture hid my neck.

'You're dying to meet this girl! Hahahaha!' I wrote.

'Hahaha! But where's your neck?' He wrote.

'I can meet this girl but can't compromise on the neck kisses. So, save the neck please!' He sent another message, adding a winking smiley.

'Hahaha! Come, suck the blood out of my neck, you vampire!' I teased.

I sent some more pictures and wrote, 'Beauty pageant portfolio by yours truly!'

As soon as I sent the pictures, I came across a pancake recipe and forwarded it to him.

'Why eat pancakes when I can have you! My edible pancake!' He replied, adding a heart emoji.

'Cheap flirting alert!' I wrote.

As I sent this message, I received a message informing me of a credit to my account. It was made by Armaan.

I immediately called him and asked angrily, "Why have you sent me this money?"

"I have already exhausted my 6 virtual sessions and I want to extend the contract," he answered calmly.

"This isn't a joke, Armaan! I'm sending the money back," I said angrily.

"But I don't understand what's wrong! It's like I want to renew my membership," he said.

"I'll sing for you whenever you want me to, but I don't want you to pay me. You're not my client anymore. You're…" I said.

"I am?" he asked.

"I mean, I'm looking forward to going on a date with you when the lockdown ends. I cannot charge you, Armaan," I said.

"But Ridhima, that would aggravate your financial problems," he said.

"No, it won't. The lockdown is about to end. I'll figure something out. I mean, we'll figure something out," I said, in a lovey-dovey voice.

To our dismay, the lockdown was extended by two more weeks, which meant that we couldn't have our first date for some more time. Armaan and I connected on video calls multiple times during the day. We ate together, cooked together, laughed together and slept together. From sharing memes to recipes to social media strategies, we made the lockdown better than our normal lives. We shared our innermost fears, long envisioned dreams and deep-seated wounds with each other. It felt like I was living the lockdown with him by my side. But despite being so close, we were far apart because I couldn't touch him. I longed to hold his hand in mine, cuddle him and hug him. I was hoping for a beautiful life after lockdown with Armaan by my side. It was one such evening when

I had connected with Armaan via video call.

"Do you remember the neighborhood uncle I told you about?" he asked.

"Yes, why?" I asked.

"He is Covid positive. He has been taken to the hospital for further examination," he said.

"Oh my god! When did he test positive?" I asked.

"I think it was yesterday," he replied.

"And who took him?" I asked.

"There's a guy who works for an NGO that helps Covid positive patients, especially those who live alone. They took him," he explained.

"Oh, that's sad," I replied.

"Yes, I wish he gets well soon," he said.

Armaan was concerned about his neighborhood uncle but had forgotten that he had been in contact with him too and thus, had high chances of being Covid positive. It was only after he got a high fever after two days that we realized that he needed to get a test done. With a fever of 102 degrees F and extreme body ache, he could barely get up when the RT-PCR report came out stating that he was Covid positive. Keshav, the same NGO guy who lived in his society, helped him with food and medicines when he was advised home isolation as his initial symptoms could be treated at home.

Armaan and I didn't stop connecting over video calls but had reduced their duration. His fever didn't subside for the first two days and he could hardly talk. His almond eyes couldn't hide his distress.

On the third night of being detected positive, Armaan suffered from acute chest pain and difficulty in breathing. He immediately called Keshav to ask for help. He was taken to the hospital without any further delay. When I woke up in the morning, I read his messages that apprised me about his condition.

'I'm going to the hospital with Keshav. I have an acute chest pain and can hardly breathe. The NGO guys will take care of me. Don't worry.' It read.

I called Armaan as soon as I read the message but he didn't pick up. I couldn't eat anything the whole day. I kept calling him after regular intervals but he didn't answer any call. I was extremely worried. I didn't even know the name of the hospital he was admitted in. Not that I could go and visit him, but I could have called the hospital management to get through him. I regretted not taking Keshav's number from him. I just wanted to know if Armaan was alright, but couldn't.

After a sleepless night of imagining the worst and chiding myself for not being positive, praying for Armaan's good health and feeling helpless about not being able to do anything, wanting to run to every hospital in Delhi-NCR to consoling myself that he would pick up the call during the day, I could connect with him in the afternoon.

"How are you? Where are you? What happened? Is it getting better?" I hurled all questions at him as soon as he picked up.

I couldn't understand what he was saying so he cut the call and texted me.

'I'm able to breathe with the help of medical oxygen. The chest pain has subsided. I am in the ICU right now.' He wrote.

'Which hospital are you admitted in? Is there anyone with you?' I replied.

'Sir Ganga Ram Hospital. Keshav stays here most of the time. If he isn't around, some other NGO guy is.' He replied.

'Can I come to meet you?' I asked.

'No, you can't step out of the house. And please don't even try to. Please take care of yourself.' He replied.

'What do the doctors say?' I asked.

'All the necessary tests have been done. I'm asked to prone at regular intervals. They are giving me medications. They can't comment on how long it will take for me to get fine because my lungs haven't started functioning properly till now. The virus has reached the lungs.' He texted.

'Hmm… Please give me Keshav's number. At least I'll have someone who can tell me about you.' I wrote.

As he shared Keshav's contact details, I video called him.

He looked like he was extremely tired and almost muttered every word he spoke. His voice wasn't clear so he used gestures to talk to me. It looked like it required everything in him to make those gestures.

I burst out crying on seeing him in that state. He tried to console me. I couldn't comprehend some of the gestures that he made. As I couldn't stop crying, I cut the video call.

'Hey, it's fine. I'll be fine soon because I still have to go on a date with you. It'll just take some time. Please don't cry. See, I am talking to you on the video call and texting you just like I used to.' He consoled.

He connected with me on a video call again and gestured that he wanted to see me smiling.

I forced a smile to which he gestured that he wanted to hug me, and clenched the fingers of both his hands together and brought them close to his heart.

When I stopped sobbing, he cut the call. He texted me that he was in touch with his parents. His parents weren't able to come to Delhi to see him but he had connected with them on video call.

He further wrote, 'I can't talk much right now. Please take care of yourself. I'll meet you soon.'

I didn't video call or message him for the rest of the day thinking that I might disturb him except once at 8 pm, but he didn't pick up.

It was Armaan's third day at the hospital. My attempts of connecting with him failed and Keshav wasn't picking up my calls. I called the hospital but they didn't get back to me with any updates about Armaan's health.

Keshav reverted to my message the next morning informing me that Armaan hadn't improved. He told me that his lungs were not healing as the infection had spread to a large extent. I asked him to save my number so that he can answer my calls.

I tried calling Armaan in the evening but his phone was switched off. His last seen on WhatsApp hadn't changed since he had last talked to me.

I called Keshav in the late evening.

"It's bad. His lungs aren't recovering. There's always someone to assist with the medicines and other requirements at the hospital. The doctors aren't able to comment on the recovery period as there are no signs as of now," Keshav said.

I laid in my bed crying for the rest of the night.

It was Armaan's fifth day in the hospital. Keshav didn't answer my calls until afternoon. He called me back in the afternoon and said,

"Armaan is no more. He had a cardiac arrest last night. The doctors couldn't save him. I've informed his parents."

I broke down as soon as I heard this. I couldn't stand on my feet any longer. I fell to the ground. I was devastated.

After days of denial, I could finally accept that I wouldn't be able to see Armaan ever again. He came into my life like an angel and brought me extreme happiness. He was a kind soul and there were not many people like him. I had hoped to start life afresh with him, but little did I know that my life was to last only till the duration of the lockdown. I had lost all hope for myself. I had lost a near one to a disease for the third time in my life. No matter how much I cried, my tears couldn't bring Armaan back, nor could my love for him. I wished that loving someone was enough to make them stay, but it wasn't.

I talked to his mother after the terrible loss they had experienced, but I knew that nothing could comfort them. They were shattered.

Ever since Armaan left, I lost all will to sing for an audience. I wanted to sing just for him. I wanted him to video call me at night asking me to sing for him once again. But that couldn't happen. Before singing exclusively for Armaan, I would vent out my pain in my songs while I lived in my head. When I started singing for Armaan, I started singing for the beauty of the art while I started living in the moment. After Armaan left, I didn't feel like singing at all. I had no drive to do anything but Armaan's wish that I shouldn't give up singing for the ones who could be healed by my songs, made me continue doing it. I didn't sing for myself anymore, but for Armaan. If it hadn't been for his wish, I would have given up on singing.

I regretted not being able to help Armaan when he needed me and not being able to be by his side during his last days. Hoping to compensate for this, I enrolled myself into an NGO that helped patients suffering from different diseases and supported their families. I dedicated my life to helping others.

About Namrata Gupta

Namrata Gupta is the author of four popular novels, 'A Silent Promise' (2015), 'The Full Circle... Stumbling Upon A Sinful Mystery' (2018), 'Together We Were (W)hole' (2020) and 'Lost Love Late Love' (2021). Her books have won many hearts.

Namrata is an English Literature graduate from Hans Raj College, Delhi University and has done her post-graduation in Masters of Business Administration from Lal Bahadur Shastri Institute of Management, Delhi. She resides in New Delhi.

'Together We Were (W)hole' was best ranked #1 in Romantic Suspense and #2 in Crime, Thriller and

Mystery on Amazon. 'Lost Love Late Love' (2021) was best ranked #3 in Romance on Amazon.

Namrata wants to make an immutable influence on the minds of the readers through her writing. She loves travelling and exploring new things. When she is not writing or travelling, you will find her interacting with her readers on social media.

Instagram: namrata511
Facebook: @authornamratagupta